THE REASON WHY

THE REASON WHY

JOHN LUCAS

Illustrations by

SARAH KIRBY

AN EYELET BOOK
an imprint of Shoestring Press

Printed by imprintdigital
Upton Pyne, Exeter
www.digital.imprint.co.uk

Typesetting and cover design by narrator typesetters and designers
www.narrator.me.uk
info@narrator.me.uk
033 022 300 39

An Eyelet Book: an imprint of Shoestring Press
19 Devonshire Avenue, Beeston, Nottingham, NG9 1BS
(0115) 925 1827
www.shoestringpress.co.uk

First published 2016
© Copyright: John Lucas
© Cover image and illustrations copyright: Sarah Kirby

The moral right of the author has been asserted.

ISBN 978-1-910323-63-2

"When stationed with the navy at Chatham, he wanted above all to paint not a heroic or grand image of conflict but the admiral's bicycle (his request was refused.)" From an essay on Eric Ravilious, *The Guardian Review*, 30 04 '11

THE REASON WHY

At 6 pm of a warm, dry, September evening in 1940, the Admiral, tall, thick-set, and dressed in mufti – caramel-coloured cords, a blue and by-no means fresh open-neck shirt worn under his visibly pilled but favourite Fairisle sleeveless sweater – left his office in **Oaktree Lodge**, a mansion on Chatham's outskirts which had been requisitioned by the War Office for naval use. As a brief respite from official cares, he intended to take a spin on his bicycle.

Before leaving, he took care to follow Service Instructions that in the event of capture by enemy forces he was to have nothing upon his person that might provide clues as to his identity. Such precautions were deemed as essential as the War Office's requirement that citizens commit to heart a password which they could unfailingly provide whenever challenged by Higher Authority to do so. For in those early days of the war there were, despite the best efforts of the RAF to repel the Luftwaffe, widespread and understandable fears of imminent invasion. The skies might for now be safe, but could the same be said of the English Channel?

The Admiral therefore placed his wallet, his identity card, and other personal items in the bottom drawer of the escritoire which had been allotted to him, then, having locked it, he hid the key beneath the potted *tradescantia* whose striped leaves graced the window embrasure of the Lodge's library, now his office.

He would be gone for no more than half-an-hour, he informed his secretary, who, in an outer office, once a drawing-room featuring three Regency-style chaise-longues, was ensconced behind a plain wooden desk (Navy issue) on which stood a table-model Remington typewriter and five colour-coded telephones from any of which, the Admiral told her, should a message for him be received, "On no account do anything, Rosie, until, that is, I return. For I", he said, finger tapping his nose and smiling mysteriously, "I alone am the Lord of Hosts."

After which, having glanced not unapprovingly at his image in the large gilt-framed mirror hanging behind his secretary's desk, he raked his fingers through the wide, if greying moustache that emphasised the firmness of his upper lip, bent, tucked his trouser bottoms into dark-blue woollen socks, then, shoulders back, strode from her presence. Pausing only to nod farewell to the front-door guard, Officer Jenks, he hoisted his portico-sheltered Raleigh with its newly acquired three-gear Sturmey-Archer fitment down four marble steps onto the gravelled drive, and having at the first attempt mounted, pedalled vigorously across the gravelled drive before disappearing from sight as he turned right along a lane that would take him toward a local feature known as Blue-Bell Hill. There, he planned to put his Sturmey-Archer gears to the test.

* * *

Ten minutes after the Admiral had left, his personal (blue) phone rang. From the lifted earpiece, which Rosie, before applying it to her ear, wiped with a cambric handkerchief whose bordering roses featured the needlepoint she had long years ago learnt at Mrs Munt's Academy of Useful Arts for Young Gentlewomen, a stertorous whisper announced "Tell the Admiral Oh Tee I thirteen for. Got it? " And the line went dead.

"Gawd knows." Officer Jenks, was frankly coarse when confided in. "Anyway, there's sod all to do till his Nibs gets back. O.T. I thirteen for, eh? Could be a cricket score. Old Trots Invincibles thirteen for … then perhaps the bloke got cut off. Unless," – he chortled, struck by a thought which he indicated by clapping a hand to his brow. "'Lord of Hosts,' eh? – "P'raps your caller meant to warn you that the Admiral's got stuck with thirteen for dinner. Can't have that, can we. Thirteen's an unlucky number. He needs to find somebody else to put on their best bib and tucker. Could be your night for a nosh, ducks!"

But Rosie indicated by a slight sniff that she did not find the officer's interpretation persuasive. Oh, T, I, thirteen for. There had to be a more convincing explanation of these mysterious words. Though as Officer Jenks rightly remarked, such explanation would have to wait upon the Admiral's return.

* * *

Meanwhile, the Admiral himself, cresting a hill in lowest gear, thumb cocked and trigger-ready to change up the better to enable free-wheeling down, ceased his whistling of "We're Off to See the Wizard" as he became sinkingly aware that all was not well beneath his buttocks, and slowing to a standstill before dismounting, saw at once that his rear tyre was, as he had feared, flat. Being however a man of parts, and used to such mishaps, he wasted no time in peevish complaint. Out from the saddle bag came his Dunlop Repair Kit tin: first the tyre, then the pink inner tube were levered off, puncture – caused by an intrusive shard of flint – located, the rubber around it dusted, adhesive patch applied, secured, inner tube and tyre forced back into position, tyre pumped up, safety-valve cap – which had been gripped between his teeth – screwed back on, and only a little after 6.30 pm, the Admiral was once more or his way, now a mere five minutes from headquarters.

* * *

Meanwhile, back at **Oaktree Lodge**, further phone calls had been received, each bearing the identical message, although the initial whisper had by now modulated in volume until it became a shout. "Tell the Admiral. *Instanter.* O.T. I THIRTEEN FOR."

"Well," Officer Jenks told an increasingly agitated Rosie, "it can't be cricket. The score'd have moved on by now. Unless, of course, rain stopped play. But this weather's general all over England." And with an upward pointing finger that reminded Rosie of Plato on the steps of the Academy as painted by Raphael, he gestured to the cloudless sky. "It must be some dinner party that's behind all this." And he smiled. "Nothing gets 'em going like thoughts of a buggered-up meal. Pardon my French.".

But Rosie, suppressing thoughts of Officer Jenks wrapped in Grecian chiton – this was no time for frivolity – at once scotched his supposition. "I have checked the Admiral's diary and, as I thought, he will be dining here. Alone," she remarked. Then, more hesitantly, "O. T. I thirteen for. Could it be code?"

"Search me" was all a chastened Jenks could say. "You'll have to ask him."

"But *how?*"

Seeing Rosie's evident distress, Officer Jenks did his best to calm her. "He'll be back soon enough," he said. "Don't you fret yourself."

* * *

Had Rose and Jenks been aware of what was happening to the Admiral, they would, however, have had cause for more than fretfulness.

Because even as they were speaking, the Admiral was running, or, to speak more accurately, wheeling, into a further difficulty. On the downhill curve of Blue-Bell Hill, where the bicycle's brakes proved less worthy than its gears, he found himself advancing rapidly and as it turned out ineluctably upon a police officer occupying the middle of the road, hand raised in requirement that the Admiral should dismount, although this proved to be a requirement which the brakes, despite the Admiral's application of them, rendered impossible.

The collision, when it came, dislodged both men, one from his saddle, the other from his feet.

"Right," the policeman said shortly, having regained an upright position from where he peered down at the face of the fallen Admiral as it flickered in an out of focus through the stroboscopic movement of the Raleigh's rear wheel. "I am Sergeant Luckhurst of Blue-Bell Hill Station."

The Admiral not replying to this, perhaps because he was intent on freeing himself from the encumbrance of his bicycle, Sergeant Luckhurst now enquired, "Are you British?" This was less polite enquiry than peremptory challenge, for the Sergeant was conscious that it was part of his duties to take responsibility for remaining at all times vigilant as to the possible infiltration of enemy agents along the Kent coast.

The Admiral's reply, when it came, being poised between growl and roar, far from satisfying the Sergeant, aroused suspicions which

were further alerted not only by the man's dress – surely a parody of a gentleman's casual garb – but by the absence of something from the bicycle's handlebar.

"So what have we here?" the Sergeant said, a note of discreet exultance in his voice. "Or rather, what *haven't* we got?" He paused significantly before answering his own question. "A man claiming, I shouldn't wonder, to be an Englishman, who is in charge of a bike **with no lamp**." Again he paused. "Despite it now being some minutes after lighting-up time." A yet further pause. "Right. You're booked." And he reached for the official notepad in the left-hand breast pocket of his tunic.

As he did so, the Admiral now himself on his feet, first took care to dust himself down, and then, with considerable hauteur, addressed his first words to the police officer.

"You forget," the Admiral said, determinedly upright despite considerable bruising to his right shin bone and, he suspected, a tear in the hinder part of his trousers, "that there is a war on, that blackout operates and that a bicycle lamp is therefore of no assistance while present conditions prevail. Besides which," he said, having reassured himself by fingertip examination that the ends of his moustache were in good order, "as even you must be aware, the sun is still high and we are enjoying broad daylight."

The Admiral's manner of speech, its hint of condescension mingled with disdain, did not find favour with the Law. "Don't you come none of that lip with me," the policeman said, "or I shall make precious short work of you."

Even as he spoke a further thought occurred, one he felt was a killer. "Besides which," he said, speaking slowly and with a modest awareness of his own acuity, "if it's broad daylight, how come you didn't see me standing in the middle of the road. Or could it be that don't they take notice of the law where you come from?"

Wherever *that* may be, he chose not to add, although the Admiral's clipped manner of speech was almost certainly part of his disguise, a trick as soon learned in Hamburg as at Harrow. So put that in your pipe and smoke it.

"I am an Admiral," the admiral said.

This being in no sense an adequate reply to the question posed, the policeman smiled sardonically.

"Proof?" he said, extending a hand.

Now, as will be recalled, the Admiral when departing from **Oaktree Lodge** had left behind all evidence of his identity. He therefore repeated, loudly this time, "Suffice it to say, that I AM AN ADMIRAL."

Sergeant Luckhurst felt his upper lip make a motion he understood to be that which in popular fiction was known as curling. "And I" he said with some asperity, "Am Alexander the Great who has had the misfortune to suffer the bolting of Beucephalus." For the Sergeant, who spent long nights in his one-man station reading literature, had recently obtained from the town's second-hand bookshop a copy of Arrianus's *Life of Alexander,* in the World's Classic Edition, and was by now familiarising himself with the Macedonian king's legendary deeds and slaughters, especially the slaughters.

* * *

Meanwhile, back at **Oaktree Lodge**, Rosie, the recipient of increasingly frantic telephone calls to report to the Admiral **I T OH THIRTEEN FOR**, was herself frantically attempting to persuade Officer Jenks that he simply *must* send a search party to locate the overdue Admiral.

* * *

And meanwhile the Admiral, having been challenged to utter his password, which in the stress of the moment he proved unable to recall, was accompanying Sergeant Luckhurst to Blue-Bell Hill police station.

"Pied Piper," the Admiral shouted as, handcuffs removed, he was locked into a cell.

In the act of turning away, Sergeant Luckhurst paused. Then, over his shoulder, he said, "Insulting a police officer in the course of his duty, is it? We'll see about that."

"Pied Piper It's my password, you …. You *officer*," the Admiral shouted. Then, once more for luck, "*Pied Piper.*" And to Sergeant Luckhurst's retreating back he called, with diminishing hope though no less authority, "I demand to see my solicitor."

But this entirely reasonable request went unheeded. Because at the very moment Sergeant Luckhurst, a man of substantial girth, reached the charge room, and before deciding whether to make the necessary phone call to a solicitor's office, he fell to the floor, dead. And there he stayed, unattended, all night.

When, next morning, his body was discovered by the in-coming day Constable, a doctor was at once summoned, who at a guess later to be confirmed by a police pathologist, identified the cause of death as a massive stroke, conceivably brought on by the Sergeant's fifty-a-day habit plus his preference for red or processed meat, including Faggots, Chitterlings and Hog's Pudding. For despite the recently imposed rationing of fresh meats which rendered them largely unobtainable by members of the public, these delicacies continued to find their way into the meat safes of the local constabulary.

The same in-coming Constable, aware of bangs and shouts emanating from the police cell, saw as he unlocked it that he was not, as he had supposed, about to free the usual far from contrite overnight drunkard, but, despite the internee's crumpled dress, a senior naval officer, indeed an Admiral whom he recognised from church ceremonies which both regularly attended.

"Blimey," the constable said as the Admiral emerged from confinement, "So *that's* where you've been hiding. A right lot of trouble *you've* caused."

"*I* have been the cause of trouble?" was as much as the Admiral could say before lapsing into apoplectic speechlessness, in which condition he can be left while we trace the cause of the Constable's sardonic words.

* * *

To return then to the previous evening. As Rosie was about to lock up for the night, a last, gabbled phone message begged her to tell the admiral to PLEASE consult the blankety blank Good Book *OR ALL WOULD BE LOST*.

Good Book? Rosie, who never left home without her pocket Bible, now realised that OT might possibly mean *Old Testament* and if so that *I* was in all likelihood the Book of *Isaiah*. As with her favourite fictional heroine, a mind like hers, once opened to suspicion, made rapid progress. She found Chapter 13, *V*erse **4**. "The Lord of Hosts mustereth the host for the battle." She touched, she admitted, she acknowledged the whole truth, one the *Shorter Oxford Dictionary,* when taken from its shelf, now confirmed. "To Muster: To assemble." The Admiral, there could be no doubt, was intended to be the recipient of orders requiring him to confront an imminent invasion. The enemy must be at the gates, or, anyway, at the port.

But where, oh, where, *was* the Admiral?

No sooner had Rosie despairingly asked herself this question than the drawing-room door opened and a man of unpleasing aspect, pistol pointing at her and plainly dressed in German uniform, advanced toward the desk uttering words which, even though ignorant of the language he spoke, Rosie knew must be a Teutonic command for her to raise her hands. There had, she was not slow to realise, been an alien landing at Chatham while the British fleet sat idle awaiting orders.

* * *

The circumstances in which a platoon, mustered by Officer Jenks, overpowered the raiding party a U Boat had put ashore with orders to advance through Chatham and to storm Naval headquarters, remain unclear, so, too, the means by which the navy was able to track the U Boat's movements. For not merely the details but the major events of that day are covered by the Official Secrets Act. Unsurprisingly, however, rumours of what was unofficially identified as "Prat's Fall" began immediate circulation in certain areas of the town and beyond. And given that in their telling and re-telling comedic aspects of the events predominated, particularly in a number of dockyard hostelries, it is understandable that, after brief deliberation, one which focussed on the need to sustain morale and respect for Authority in the armed services, the Admiral's bicycle was considered, even by the Admiral himself, to be a subject altogether unsuitable for artistic depiction in a time of war.